STU

Weekly Reader Children's Book Club presents

# The Giants' Farm

# The Giants' Farm

by *JANE YOLEN*

*pictures by*
TOMIE DE PAOLA

A *Clarion Book*
The Seabury Press • New York

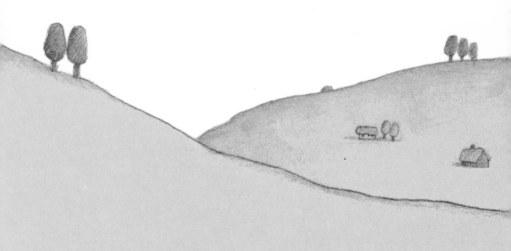

*For my little giant*
JASON

The Seabury Press, 815 Second Avenue,
New York, New York 10017
Text copyright © 1977 by Jane Yolen
Illustrations copyright © 1977 by Tomie de Paola
Printed in the United States of America

*Library of Congress Cataloging in Publication Data*

Yolen, Jane H.     The giants' farm.     "A Clarion book."
Summary: A group of distinctly different giants have problems
to solve when they decide to live together on a farm.
[1. Giants—Fiction. 2. Farm life—Fictional] I. De Paola,
Thomas Anthony. II. Title.
PZ7.Y78Gi     [E]     76-58317     ISBN 0-8164-3193-0

# Contents

# 1. The Farm

Long ago there were five giants who wanted to live together on a farm.

There was Grizzle. He was the biggest.

And Stout, who was fat.

There were the twins, Grab and Grub.

And the little giant Dab.

First they had to clear the land. Grizzle
picked up huge boulders. He laid them one
on top of another for a wall.

Together Grab and Grub moved trees.
Dab raked everything smooth.
And Stout made something to eat.

Then they had to build a fine big house
of wood. It had to be just the right size for
five giants.

Grab and Grub sawed the beams.

Grizzle put on the roof.

Dab gave out the nails.

And Stout made something to eat.

Then they had to furnish the house.
They had to find things just the right size for
five giants.

Grizzle brought in the couch and chairs
and a great grandfather clock.

Grab and Grub moved in the grand
piano.

Dab carried in the platters and mugs.

And Stout made something to eat.

At last they sat down to dinner.

Dab said, "Now we have a farm of our very own. What shall we call it?"

"How about naming it George?" said Grizzle.

Little Dab sighed. "That's not poetic," he said.

"How about Our Home?" asked the twins together.

Little Dab sighed. "That's too plain."

"How about Pudding Place?" said Stout, licking his lips.

No one paid any attention to him.

"Well, you do not like George or Our Home or Pudding Place," growled Grizzle. The others growled along with him. "What do you like?"

"That I don't know," said Little Dab. "But it will come."

In the middle of dinner, Dab looked up. He smiled. "I have it," he said. "The very best name for a giants' place."

They all looked at him.

Little Dab raised his cup. "Fe-Fi-Fo-Farm," he said.

"Sounds good to me," all the others said.

And so their farm was named.

# 2. The Secret

Grab and Grub had a secret. They had a secret together.

When any other giant had a secret, he had it to himself. One giant, one secret.

But Grab and Grub were twins. They were so much alike, they were like one person.

If Grab was happy, Grub was happy. If Grub was sad, Grab was sad.

So when one of them had a secret, they both had a secret. It was just their way.

This time it was a big secret. A giant of a secret. And they swore they would not tell.

Grab ran up to Grizzle. "We have a secret," he said.

Grizzle growled and hammered a nail. "What is your secret?"

"We won't tell," said Grab.

Grizzle growled. The nail went in with one pound.

Grub went up to Stout. "We have a secret," he said.

Stout frowned and ate a melon. "What is your secret?"

"We won't tell," said Grub.

Stout sighed and ate another melon.

Grab and Grub ran up to the little giant Dab. "We have a secret," they said.

Dab looked up from his book. "I cannot hear you," he said.

Grab shouted, "We have..."

Grub shouted, "...a secret!"

Dab put his hand to his ear. He said quietly, "I am the smallest giant. I have the smallest ears. Small ears cannot hear loud sounds. I cannot hear what you are trying to tell me."

Grab looked at Grub.

Grub looked at Grab.

"We are not telling you anything," they said. "It is our secret and we will not tell."

"I cannot hear you in my little ears," said Dab. He looked down at his book again.

Grab ran to one side.

Grub ran to the other.

They whispered in both of Dab's little ears.

"We will not tell you that today is our birthday," they said, "because it is a secret."

Dab took Grab and Grub by the hands. "Happy birthday," he said.

"How did you guess that was our secret?" asked the twins. But they were really very pleased that he knew.

Dab smiled. "I'll never tell."

# 3. Stout's Candy

Stout wanted to eat. Stout always wanted to eat.

But today the cookie jar was empty.

"I will have to make something," said Stout. "I will have to make something good to eat."

He got out a bowl.

He got out a cookbook.

He turned to the candy page. "Giant No-Cook Bon-bons," he read. "That sounds good."

He looked at the picture in the book. It made him hungry. He looked at the recipe.

2 tbsp. butter
1/8 tsp. vanilla
10 tbsp. confectioner's sugar
3/4 C. chopped nuts

Stout scratched his head. "I do not know how to get these," he said. "I do not know what a *tbsp* is. I do not know what a *tsp* is. I have never heard of a *C*."

23

Stout sat down at the table and cried. He cried great big giant tears. They fell off his nose and rolled into the bowl.

Soon the bowl was filled with tears.

"What are you doing?" asked the little giant Dab.

"I am making something to eat," said Stout with a sniff.

"It looks as if you are making something to drink," said Dab. But he said it with a kind smile.

"I want to make Giant No-Cook Bon-bons," said Stout. "But I cannot do it." He pointed to the book.

Dab read the recipe. "Do we have butter?"

"Yes," said Stout.

"Do we have the right kind of sugar?" asked Dab.

"Yes," said Stout.

"Do we have vanilla and nuts?" asked Dab.

"Yes and yes," said Stout.

"Then what is wrong?"

Stout began to sniff again. "I do not have a *tbsp* or a *tsp* or a *C*," he said.

Dab put his head to one side. "A *tbsp* or a *tsp* or a *C*?"

"Yes," said Stout. He pointed to the page. "And there they are."

Dab began to laugh. It was not a nasty laugh. It was a nice laugh. "I will show you what those are," he said.

He took a pencil and wrote in Stout's book.

### Giant No-Cook Bon-bons

TABLESPOONS
2 tbsp. butter

teaspoon
1/8 tsp. vanilla

TABLESPOONS
10 tbsp. confectioner's sugar

CUP
3/4 C. chopped nuts

Stout followed the recipe. In an hour he was done.

He was so pleased, he invited the other giants to share his candy. He gave them each one. That left eight for Stout.

When he was finished, he was quite full. He only had room left for dinner.

# 4. Grizzle's Grumble

It was a gray day. The giants were all at home.

Grizzle began to grumble. No one listened to him. He grumbled louder. Still no one heard. At last he began to sing a grumbling song:

"I do not like being big.
I do not like being big.
I fall and break things,
I cannot make things,
I do not like being big."

29

This time the other giants heard him.

"You are right," said Stout. "It is no fun being big. A big hand gets stuck in the cookie jar."

This made Grizzle even sadder. He sang his grumble even louder.

"I do not like being big.
I do not like being big.
Nothing fits right,
Nothing sits right,
I do not like being big."

"You are right," said Grab.
"You are right," said Grub.

Then Grab said, "If you are big, you get all the hand-me-ups. Like the socks that have lost their elastic."

And Grub added, "And the sweaters that are all stretched out."

Grizzle felt worse and worse. His chin fell to his chest. His mouth pulled down. Two big tears started in his eyes. He tried to sing his grumble again. All that came out was:

"I do not ... *blub* ... *blub* ... *blub*."

Little Dab came into the room. "I have a *big* problem."

"I have a *big* problem, too," said Grizzle. "And it's me." He began to *blub* ... *blub* ... *blub* again.

"My big problem is that I am not big enough," said Dab. "I cannot reach the book I want. It is on the very top shelf."

"I will get it," said Grab, but he could not reach.

"I will get it," said Grub, but he could not reach.

Stout wiped his mouth. "I would try to get it for you," he said, reaching for another candy. "But if Grab cannot get it and Grub cannot get it, then I cannot get it either."

"Oh dear," said Dab. "This is a *bigger* problem than I thought."

Grizzle stopped crying. He looked at the
high shelf where Dab was pointing. Then he
got up. And up. And up. He got the book and
handed it to Dab.

Dab smiled up at Grizzle. "I don't know what I would do without some really big friends around," he said. "I can solve the *little* problems myself. But for *big* problems, you need a friend."

Grizzle thought about that a moment. Then he smiled.

The sun came out. It was no longer a gray day.

# 5. And Little Dab

Snow fell on the giants' farm for a day and a night. No one could go out.

So Grizzle slept. He dreamed wonderful dreams.

Stout ate. He ate and ate. He ate wonderful eats.

Grab and Grub giggled and talked. They told each other wonderful things. Riddles and jokes and rhymes.

But Little Dab was bored.

He looked out of the window. All he could see was snow and snow and more snow.

"I liked it in the spring," said Little Dab. "That was when we made the farm. We made the farm and planted our garden. I liked it then," said Dab.

"ZZZZZZZZZ" said Grizzle.

"I liked it in the summer," said Little Dab. "That was when we weeded our garden. We weeded it and watched it grow. I liked it then," said Dab.

"MUNCH" said Stout.

"And I liked it in the fall," said Little Dab. "That was when we picked our garden. We cooked and canned the things from our garden. We made our garden ready for its long winter sleep. I liked it then," said Dab.

"GIGGLE GIGGLE," said Grab and Grub.

"Yes," said Little Dab, and he looked out of the window. "I liked it in the spring and summer and fall. I liked making something out of nothing. But I do not like winter at all. There isn't anything to do."

Grizzle opened one eye. "You need to dream," he said. "And winter is just right for dreaming." Then he closed his eye and fell asleep again.

Stout stopped between bites. "You need to fill yourself with something sweet," he said. "Winter is just right for that." He closed his mouth. He continued chewing.

Grab and Grub looked at one another. They giggled. "Make up riddles and jokes and rhymes," they said. "They always help to pass the time. And winter has plenty of time to pass." They giggled again.

Little Dab turned away. He was very sad. Each of the other giants had something. But he had nothing. Nothing to do. Except watch the snow.

One flake.

Two flakes.

It kept on snowing.

Little Dab thought about dreaming. He thought about eating. He thought about rhymes. He thought about sleeping and filling and telling. He thought and thought about making something from nothing.

"I HAVE IT," he shouted in Grizzle's ear.

Grizzle kept on sleeping.

"I HAVE IT," he shouted into Stout's open mouth.

Stout kept on eating.

"I HAVE IT," he sang in between Grab
'and Grub's giggles.

They kept on playing.

Little Dab ran to the desk. He took out a
piece of paper and a pencil. He sat down by
the window. He did not look at the snow.

Grizzle sat up. Stout stopped eating. Grab and Grub forgot their game. "What do you have?" they all asked.

"I will show you," said Little Dab. "It is a dream. It is filling and sweet. It is full of rhymes."

Dab put the paper before him. He took up the pencil. He began to write:

*Long ago there were five giants who wanted to live together on a farm....*

A recipe for you to make

## *Stout's Giant No-Cook Bon-bons*

2    tablespoons butter
⅛    teaspoon vanilla
10   tablespoons confectioner's sugar
¾    cup chopped nuts

1. Take butter out of the refrigerator. Let it get soft.

2. Mash the butter with a spoon. Keep mashing it. It will look like whipped cream.

3. Mix the vanilla in one drop at a time.

4. Add the sugar to the butter and vanilla mixture. Add it slowly, one spoonful at a time. Mix and mix and mix some more.

5. Add the chopped nuts a few nuts at a time. Mix and mix and mix some more.

6. Take a large pinch of the mixture with your fingers. Roll it in a ball. Take another, make another. And another. Make twelve balls in all. Put all the balls on a plate that is lined with wax paper.

7. Put the plate with the candy balls in the refrigerator. Let them get hard.

8. If you want to, you can pour melted sweetened chocolate over these candies. Then they will really be *bon-bon*. That is French for good-good.

9. Eat.